Charles H Collins

Echoes from the Highland Hills

Charles H Collins

Echoes from the Highland Hills

ISBN/EAN: 9783743349063

Manufactured in Europe, USA, Canada, Australia, Japa

Cover: Foto ©Andreas Hilbeck / pixelio.de

Manufactured and distributed by brebook publishing software (www.brebook.com)

Charles H Collins

Echoes from the Highland Hills

ECHOES

FROM THE

HLAND HILLS.

BY

CHARLES H. COLLINS,

Of the Hillsboro (Ohio) Bar.

CINCINNATI:

PETER G. THOMSON, PUBLISHER,

1884.

INSCRIPTION.

To those Friends at whose Request these Selectio
from Various Contributions to the Press, in
Various Places, have been Grouped
together, this Unpretending
Volume is
Dedicated by the Author,
who has for so Many Years Lived
with them in this Beautiful Section of our Sta

C. H. COLLINS.

Hillsboro, Ohio, 1881.

CONTENTS.

ADDENDA.

(vi)

ECHOES

FROM THE

Highland Hills.

IN MEMORIAM.

HE is not dead. He could not die,
　His spirit has returned to God;
What cares that *soul*, released and free,
　For mouldering body 'neath the sod?

The body dies: an empty shell,
　It fills the dark and cheerless grave;
The *mind*, immortal, upward soars,
　No longer bound to earth *a slave*.

They made his grave 'mid drifting snow,
　While sadly blew the north-wind's breath,
And hid from sight that noble heart,
　So calm, so still, —they call it death.

All were his friends, the loved, *not* lost,
　And o'er the cold and pulseless clay
The tears of grief in anguish fall;
　The drops of sorrow, naught can stay.

NOTE.—A tribute to Cyrus B. Trimble, a young attorney of the Hillsborough (O.) Bar, of great promise and every excellent quality. He died in the Winter of 1866-7, and his death was regretted by all, and by none more than the writer.　　　　　　　　　　　(9)

IN MEMORIAM.

He is not dead. He could not die,
  His spirit has returned to God;
What cares that *soul*, released and free,
  For mouldering body 'neath the sod?

The body dies: an empty shell,
  It fills the dark and cheerless grave;
The *mind*, immortal, upward soars,
  No longer bound to earth *a slave.*

They made his grave 'mid drifting snow,
  While sadly blew the north-wind's breath,
And hid from sight that noble heart,
  So calm, so still, —they call it death.

All were his friends, the loved, *not* lost,
  And o'er the cold and pulseless clay
The tears of grief in anguish fall;
  The drops of sorrow, naught can stay.

Note.—A tribute to Cyrus B. Trimble, a young attorney of the Hillsborough (O.) Bar, of great promise and every excellent quality. He died in the Winter of 1866-7, and his death was regretted by all, and by none more than the writer.   (9)

O stricken mortals, let our pride
  Bow humbly to the will of fate;
No cry, from torn or broken hearts,
  Can pass where glows the golden gate.

We ponder o'er the silent tomb
  Where his young manhood meets decay;
Shall we forget the 'raptured soul,
  Now bright'ning in eternal day?

To bring him back, Ah! who would wish
  To loose the earthly, fragile shroud,
And place again this pure, young heart
  In contact with the world's vile crowd.

Let mem'ry, with its magic charm,
  Beguile us into perfect trust,
And Hope, still beck'ning upward, point
  While musing on the hidden dust.

Cease idle tears, the dull, cold ear
  Is deaf for aye to praise or blame;
"The God who gave has ta'en away,
  And blessed be His holy name."

A BORDER RAID. (1863.)

I

FROM the gray depths of Ozark's height,
At the red dawn of morning light,
While all the air with music filled,
And forest birds their anthems trilled,
One Summer morn, of glorious sky,
Of fragrant breeze, and ripple's sigh,
When green the dewy clover sprung,
And blooming flowers their perfume flung,
Adown the mountain's caverned side
The iron warriors of SHELBY ride,
Led by a chief with haughty crest,
Who, o'er Missouri's verdant plain,
Had gazed in dreary exile vain,
Yet hoped and longed to cross again.
And now intent on deadly raid,
At column's van his flag displayed,
He dooms the prairies fair shall see
The march of border chivalry,
And test, in battle's fierce alarms,
The vaunted power of northern arms.

Note.—Gen. Joseph O. Shelby was the Marion of the Confederacy in the Trans-Mississippi department. His campaigns are described in ornate and glowing style by his Adjutant, Major John C. Edwards, in a work called "Shelby and his Men." It is but just to say that these "Raids," of which there were many, accomplished no good purpose.

II

Now near Neosho's pebbled stream
The leader ponders o'er the dream .
That once again in fair array
He'll reach his home: *but can he stay?*
Now from the densest óaken arch
Echoes the war cry, "Forward, March."
Come, gallop, dash o'er leagues of grass,
Cross forest, slough and deep morass,
Thread tangled thicket and thorny brake,
Pass rushing river and placid lake,
'Till, in the broad Missouri's wave,
Each warrior stoops his brow to lave,
And from its shifting, sandy brink
Each trusty steed may freely drink.
Where are your homes?   Alas! no more,
The echoes from the voiceless shore
Proclaim the hopeless, future state
Of hearth-stones drear and desolate,
And by the dark and turbid waters,
Behold Missouri's mourning daughters!
Forget the weary, wildering miles,
Restore their beauty, joy and smiles.
Now charge the host by Luna's gleams,
Now fight him by Apollo's beams,
Nor spare on hated foreign foe
The bayonet thrust or sabre blow.

Count not the battle lost or won,
Until your desperate task is done.

III

At bugle call, and tap of drum,
The ardent youth to SHELBY come,
And 'neath his banner's oft-tried might,
Fight for the cause *they* deem is right,
While tyrants first begin to fear,
The clanging of a Southern spear,
And in their guilty slumbers see
Visions of SHELBY's warriors free,
'Till 'roused by cannon's dreaded fire,
They know that now the vengeful ire
Of Exile's hearts, and Exile's steel,
In their own persons they shall feel,
And in their wasted homes shall know
How sad has been the Exile's woe,
And with their blood shall well repay
The pillage, plunder and foray,
The reckless license, death and smart,
Inflicted on Missouri's heart.
Let terror reign, why should it not?
Can such injustice be forgot?
What other measure can they crave,
Of Southern men, *than that they gave?*

IV

What stirs the State so far and wide,
From Merrimac to Kansas side;
From Osage down to Gasconade—
What but the fame of Shelby's raid?
The skulker, from his downy bed,
In coward haste has sprang and fled,
While from the hostile camps afar,
The Federals rush to join the war,
And fierce and fast comes death below—
The ancient town of Girardeau,
And musket shot and batteries' peal
O'er Pilot Knob in echoes steal;
The Iron Mountain hears report,
How 'round its base Death holds his court;
The Capital sees the meteor flash,
As by the walls its squadrons dash,
And hears the spiteful cannon's roar,
Resounding from the leafy shore.
Fair Boonville opens wide her gate,
To welcome the hero saved by fate.
The gentle city, Arrow-Rock,
Feels now the Federal's battle shock,
And beauteous plains of calm Saline
And shelving banks of dark Lamine:
Here, stern and harsh were war's decrees,
Where men, unyielding as the trees

'Mid which they fought—that awful day—
Made of themselves the vultures' prey.
The stream is blood! O horrid sight,
Hide it from vision, welcome night
And welcome morn; let Marshall view
SHELBY's shattered band pass through.

V

Now fast on SHELBY's straggling rear,
O'er brake, and waste and prairies drear,
The gathering clans from every post
Press on. In truth a mighty host;
At morn these boasting foemen said,
"Our lines are closely 'round him spread;
Now friendly Parcea, draw the net;
SHELBY, alas! thy sun is set!"
But trust not fate, your game is lost;
Ah! had you counted but the cost,
And spared the prairies' fitful gales,
Your beaten, baffled, dying wails,
And corpses scattered through the wood,
Trampled with iron hoof in blood;
And by the evening's purple light,
Stark, stiff and ghastly to the sight.
The wounded hear the sabres ring,
And ceaseless, tireless clattering
Of hoof after hoof, on prairie sod,
As SHELBY plies his deadly rod.

Now Waverly sees his banners fly,
Reflected in the sun-set sky;
Young city, nestled in the bluff,
Destined ere long to usage rough.
Behold in lonely streets arrayed
The rent and war-worn young Brigade, —
'Twas SHELBY's home. He lingered yet,
Too long 'mid scenes he can't forget.
In its defense he could but die,
From household gods he would not fly,
'Though all around his Spartan band
The circling foemen grimly stand.
Here, for the last, he turns at bay;
He fights, he conquers, wins the day,
And 'scapes the meshes, nets and toils,
'Mid tumult, bloodshed and turmoils,
To come in after days once more,
And shock again the Federal power.

VI

Through Dover streets his horsemen rush,
And penetrate dark Tabo's brush;
Great Lexington, the County's queen,
Beholds her favorites' glitt'ring sheen.
Then westward bends, like bird or wind,
Leaves dull pursuit far, far behind;
A score of leagues from morn 'till eve,
Behind each day, his horsemen leave;

And Kansas borders far and near
Felt SHELBY's unrelenting spear.
Her cities burned with lurid flame,
Sad vengeance for Missouri's shame.
Yet could he but retaliate
The wrongs done his adopted State ?
Arkansas safely reached at last,
The Brigade rests, its labors past.
Yet long in verse or sadder prose
Shall live the history of its woes,
And prairies green, and forest shade,
Keep fast the mem'ry of the Raid.

MISSOURI.

(ANTE-BELLUM.)

It seems to me a pleasant dream,
Of forest, prairie and gentle stream:
Each day was golden, joy crown'd the night;
The skies all sunny, the moon all bright.
Then, all was peace and joy within,
Thy borders wide, O fair Saline;
And War had ne'er, in sweeping wrath,
Sown discord in each well-known path,
And left thy homesteads sad and low,—
Mementoes of a deadly woe.

Let Fancy glide o'er Waconda,
Or tread thy vast expanse, Teetsaw;
Or when the autumn suns are fine,
In Salt-Fork cast the angler's line;
Or near its cool sequestered haunts,
Watch soaring geese or screaming brants;
Or as the whirring wood-grouse spring,
With shot-gun "take them on the wing"
Or cross the turbid river's tide,
To thickets dense, by water side;
With horse and hound, from coverts near
Beat up the red-fox, 'rouse the deer;

NOTE—The writer was a resident of western Missouri (while a young man) for five years.

Follow the grouse o'er field and plain,
Nor deem it labor all in vain,
'Though dogs may tire in endless race
And sportsmen fail in long, long chase.
Do you note that spot in Heaven's blue,
Where sand cranes sing 'ere lost to view,
And soaring sing, obscured from sight,
In dread Empyrean's lonely height ?
See how the wild geese face the wind,
And leave pursuers far behind ;
Wedge-like and arrowy, cut the breeze,
And wing their flight with grace and ease.

On sentinel trees, by forest gate,
The watchful hawks in patience wait
For ambushed quails, or nestling hare,
To venture from their grassy lair :
A rustle, then a light'ning flash,
The hawk has made a sudden dash—
He bears aloft the trembling game,
To kill for food, and *not* for fame.

'Tis twilight now by lakelet's edge,
The wild duck parts the cluster'd sedge,
Thick and coarse, tall and rank;
It grows by lake-side dark and dank.
The Pelican, with double throat,
And Swan, with wild and whistling note,

Now join in chorus far and near,
In sounds confused on list'ning ear,
While from the slough and gloamy fen,
Spring the wood-cock and water-hen.

And o'er the deep and wide morass,
In zig-zag flights, the Jack Snipe pass;
The Dove's low voice is heard remote,
And rattlesnake's death-warning note;
The night-owl, from the forests still,
Responds unto the Whip-poor-will,
While o'er the purpling, fading day
The pale moon sheds her placid ray.
Grim spectres peer in leafy shades,
And dancing lights on prairie glades,
As starting from the azure dome,
The stars step forth to guide us home.

By beaten tracks, see all around
The hemp stands thickly on the ground,
And in the verdant pastures close
The broad-horned cattle seek repose.
Now stirs the bearded, ripening wheat,
And perfume comes from meadows sweet;
And proudly waves the tasseling corn,
And Plenty fills her bounteous horn.
The orchards bend beneath their load
Along each lane and public road;

And grapes, as famed for sparkling wine
As those which grace the banks of Rhine ;
And luscious plums as large and sound
As e'er on Syrian plains are found ;
Peach and cherry and wild crab trees,
Emitting fragrance on the breeze ;
Plants of all shades and every dye,
To suit the taste or please the eye.

Through foliage dense there glows a light
From negro cabins glist'ning white ;
This greets the eye, while on the sense
Fall banjo tones in sweet cadence.
On still night air there rise and fall
The notes of ballads musical ;
And on the cabin floor resounds
Reels, jigs, or far more famed "break-downs."
O happy race, your joys are past !
Your long-sought freedom, reached at last,
Has brought along in endless train
Disease, and hunger, death and pain.

And do you know this fairy land ?
And would you in its portals stand ?
And day by day your praises give,
If there you might in quiet live,
And on its charming prairie sod,
"From nature, look to nature's God ?"

What shall, Missouri, be thy fate,
The mighty western Empire State,
Who 'mid thy sisters ranks as high
As Venus in the starry sky?

———

ANNO SIXTY-NINE.

CHRONOS or Saturn, as the poets feign,
In ages bygone held his mystic reign,
Before Olympus rose, or the golden earth
To monstrous lies and shams had given birth;
Chief of the elder gods, a fabled race,
He ruled supreme in boundless realms of space.
The world was new, and no distempered schemes
Had marred its beauty, or disturbed its dreams—
Fit habitation for the gods above,
A scene of quiet, innocence and love—
'Till envious Fate pronounced the harsh decree,
That this Elysium should cease to be,
And, in its stead, should be intestine wars,

NOTE.—Extract from New Year's Address, Jan. 1, 1870.

From nation's quarrels down to family jars.
On Eden's plain the stars, that awful day,
Looked down upon the man of clay,
Save one of ruddy hue, Bellona styled,
Who gazed upon the horrid scene and smiled;
And fiercely blazed the harbinger of woe,
When brother died by brother's angry blow.
Then Crime began, and centuries to roll
Their floods of anguish o'er the human soul.
Year follows year, though life is but a span,
And Time continues, as it first began,
Remorseless, unrelenting and a king,
Whose craving maw devours each mortal thing;
Even his own offspring—days, years and hours—
Succumb before the destroyer's powers.
The eras gone before are soon forgot,
Their doom unheeded, for "they are not."
Hear ye that knell? it is the midnight chime
Tolling the death of latest child of Time.
The faded year, decrepit, and forlorn,
Yields up its breath, and *Seventy* is born.
Come welcome, friends, with a rousing cheer,
The rush to life of the glad New Year,
As purple dawn peers o'er the Highland Hill,
The happy voices all the morning fill.
Hopeful New Year, thy young and blooming face
Recks not or cares not for thy sire's disgrace.
That hoary Titan, plunged in every vice,

Whose trumps were knaves, and weapons loaded
    dice;
A desperate gamester, "who palmed his hand,"
No oath could bind him, no promise stand.
A black career, yet touched by fitful rays,
The gleaming promises of better days,
When Freedom's banner shall float in azure sky,
And tyrants tremble, sicken, fall and die.
A bastard brood from ignorance allowed
To rule and plunder the great gaping crowd,
Who judge of merit by the purse alone,
And needing bread, are content with a stone.
No wonder philosophers leave us in doubt,
Whether we should weep, or laugh right out,
At witnessing the follies of human grubs,
Who are partly snobs and partly scrubs.
Our text is short: the wild antics crazy
Of Sixty-Nine, *requiescat in pace*,
Which means, no matter what, it fits the rhyme
Of this *annus mirabilis* of crime.
By lake, and river, mountain, sea and wood,
The stains are red with horrid hue of blood,
And through the long drawn months, 'neath
    ev'ry sky,
Constant and causeless murders shock the eye.
They call it *war*, these fighting despots all,
Who strive their fellows to kill or enthrall.
It matters little who may win, for still

The masters on the *Canaille* work their will;
Treat men as cattle, fit but to be slaves,
Or, food for powder, fill ignoble graves.
These mongrel wretches, sport of idle kings,
The tools of knaves, perhaps voting *things;*
Things for a Lopez, or the smarter beasts,
To use as purveyors for daily feasts,
And while content to pick the well cleaned bones.
Serve as *substratum* for their master's thrones.
So it has been; so it will ever be;
On this great fact all histories agree,—
The many serve the purpose of a few,
Who claim all honors as their own just due.
Though this was disputed by our great sires,
Whose faith was tested in the battle fires,
And came forth, unsullied, from burning coals,
The hopeful anchor to their noble souls.

VESPERS.

Alone upon this tufted hill
    In silence, while the air
Is pulseless, all is still, so still,
    You feel no presence there.
But hark, from distant village tow'r
    Saint Mary's gentle strain
Proclaims the blessed vesper hour,—
    Tired Labor rests again.

The mellowed tones, in liquid chime,
    Fall on the list'ning ear;
Down drop the spades, comes vesper time.
    Then home with all its cheer.
O! weary life, with short respite,
    All work and restless brain;
For labor hard each morn's red light
    Brings fast upon its train.

The sun's last rays from western sky
    Glint on Saint Mary's spire;
The cross, all golden, sparkles high
    With streams of burnished fire.
Great bars of purple and yellow light
    Reach to the zenith blue,

Note—From Muntz hill, overlooking the highway leading from Hillsboro to Belfast.

As day fades into sullen night,
  Show dying dolphins' hue.

All ripened are the glowing fields,
  Down drops the dew on earth;
We see the fruitful harvest yields,
  For Labor gave it birth.
From sheltered nooks the cabin fires
  Ascending, make us feel
That woman's hand, which never tires,
  Prepares the evening meal.

By coverts close, and brook-side lone,
  The cattle stand in peace,
And twilight beetles' soothing drone
  Now murmurs, Labor, cease;
On dusty road, far, far below,
  The trav'lers hurry by,
Like phantom horsemen flitting go,
  Where home and pleasures lie.

O blessed, blessed eventide,
  When vesper hymns arise,
And Labor lays its toils aside,
  And turns to God its eyes;
Who has not felt in this sweet hour,
  Whate'er his trials were,
That time would come, no earthly power
  Could bring again despair?

OPENING OF MUSIC HALL.

(HILLSBORO, OHIO.)

WHERE erst the *Shawnees* roved, we meet to-night,
　　But wigwam smoke nor piercing whoop are here;
Bright eyes their gentlest radiance shed around,
　　And hearts, most timid, throb without a fear.
The hall we dedicate need not compare
　　With old world piles of centuries renown;
They speak of wealth, of skill, and art most rare,
　　But are they not with crime and wrong o'er-
　　　　grown?
Egyptian slaves might rear a mass of stone,
　　To lure some lonely wand'rer into thought,
But *here* no jackals prowl; Time holds his scythe,
　　And blue-eyed youth prevails, nor feareth aught;
No monarch rules, save in the realms of taste,
　　And Jew and Gentile, in the long-sought hall,
May, like the chorus, to the banquet haste,—
　　So dividends are promptly paid on call.
Here wit and jocund mirth shall hold their court,
　　And soul-full music cheat old Time of care;
The tripping feet at evening hours shall laugh,
　　And gray-beard wisdom in its pleasures share.
The lover here his cunning wiles shall spread,

NOTE—Part of a spoken address at dedication of the hall, January 14,
1871. The hall has served its day, and a new Opera House is now
contemplated, and will, *perhaps*, be erected.

The artless maiden list with captive will;
The sober student here shall raise his head,
  And careless childhood drink its blessed fill.
The politician here his web shall weave,
  And honest yeomen swallow all he says,—
Now wonder at his lies, or sadly grieve
  To hear his partial blame or fulsome praise.
Here head-manipulators show their chart,
  And while they feel each grinning urchin's head,
Find in each bump a cultivated heart,
  And draw his future as a statesman bred.
The unrolled panorama here shall work
  On boys and girls its ever-potent spell.
The frolic minstrel wear his sable mark,
  And tell the jokes we all remember well.
The gentle Spring, warm Summer's modest tear,
  The russet Autumn, with its mournful wind,
The Vicking Winter, too, shall find us here
  To stir the backward pulse and cheer the mind.
Now on the hall may peace her rays reflect,
  May honest labor find its solace here;
May truth her crystal pillars here erect,
  With many a fervent, ardent worshipper.
So where the Shawnee roved and pitched his tent,
  We meet, as often may we meet again,
And in this hall find unalloyed content,
  Without a thought of guile or throb of pain.
Here, as we try the tedious hours to while,

As amateurs upon the mimic stage,
May we but ask for beauty's partial smile,
   Nor raise the ire of philosophic age.
All worldly things must end : so does my verse,
   Would it were worthier of a worthy cause;
But "what is writ is writ," it might be worse,
   For rhymes agree not with our crabbed laws.
The modest muse we oft may woo in vain,
   As hard to win as fabled Orient bride;
The siren lingers in the dewy plain,
   Or haunts the lonely mountain's side.
The coy enchantress flees from lover rude,
   And lurks in coverts with the sylvan pan,
While hidden nymphs, from densest solitude,
   Echo the cry, *"Come, catch her if you can."*

THE ORIOLE.

HAUNTER of the orchard,
  Singing clear and free,
Flitting o'er the green sward,
  Full of melody,
Where the apple blossoms, or buds the tulip tree.

In the blush of morning,
  In the evening gray,
Ever still adorning
  All the Summer's day.
From thy airy mansion, with the winds at play.

Challenging the plough boy,
  "Whistling his team afield,"
With thy matin song of joy,
  All his sense to yield
To the mocking banter, from bending willow shield.

Flecked in brightest yellow,
  Helmeted in black,
Piping thy whistle mellow,
  Glancing on his track,
Like a gnome or fairy, tempting answer back.

NOTE—The colors of the Calverts were black and orange. The Oriole, which has the same markings, was hence called "The Baltimore Oriole." The English sparrow has driven the beautiful Fire-bird away from most localities.

Delicate vermillion,
Dancing on the sight,
Deepest tinge of orange
In thy plumage bright,
Lend beauty to the foliage, and sparkle in the light

These are the colors olden,
Of lordly Baltimore,
Flashed by the Fire-bird golden,
Upon our western shore,
And giving thee a title, which noble Calverts bore

Among the branches gleaming,
This heraldic coat of arms,
Like ancient banner streaming,
But adds unto thy charms,
Linked with the noble Calverts and Indian alarms.

The Baltimores are sleeping,
The sponsors of thy name,
But *thy* presence still is keeping,
Eternally their fame,
Undying and immortal, like Roman Vestal's flame.

WHAT'S IT ALL WORTH?

WITH fevered brain I stood, one Summer day,
  Where the rustling grass, in requiem moan,
Its dirges chanted o'er the crumbling clay,
  Of one whose yearning soul was like mine own,
Whose burning hopes mapped out his life career,
  With glowing visions of success to be,
Whose thrilling voice was to the list'ning ear
  Like trumpet's call to certain victory.

He thought: he toiled; and yet to all was seen,
  As the years passed on, in life's fitful dreams,
That much he loved blue skies and fields of green,
  And the murmuring fall of purling streams,
The breath of Spring, warm Summer's fervid kiss,
  The trailing vines, in clustering wood and wold,
The song of birds and childhood's artless bliss,
  To him were studies as life's current rolled.

Ambition lured him with its tempting fruit,
  Its mirage fair and bright imagined land,
Which changed to phantoms in his hot pursuit,
  Or left but ashes in his clinging hand.
Nor did his honors to him joy or love,
  Contented mind or dove-eyed peace e'er bring;
But cares were set upon his wrinkled brow
  Ere yet had swiftly passed his youth's glad Spring.

By the sickly light of the midnight lamp,
　　In books of strange device, he longing sought
To learn that Lore no poverty could damp,
　　Or try to fathom what no book had taught.
'Mid the myriad stars he oft would peer,
　　Or pensive gaze on bush, and brook and hill,
While all along the earth there moved a fear,
　　A deep, sad voice which to him boded ill.

One night a zephyr floated from the sky,
　　And whispering said, "O searching son of earth,
Not long for thee remains the hopeless sigh,
　　The quest to know *What all this life is worth;*
Then through his quickened frame like lightning
　　crept
　　A pain, and the heart was forever still;
The student toiler 'neath the moist grass slept,
　　The soul, untrammeled, roamed all space at will.

IN THE TWILIGHT.

(TO MY WIFE.)

I.

In the fleecy haze,
'Mid sunset rays,
The clouds empurpled, the sky of gold,
As day expires,
In twilight fires,
O what do thine eyes, sweetheart, behold?

II.

Where the sky is dark,
A glittering spark,
A signal point in the depths afar ;
The jet night's lamp,
To her speckled camp,
And the pale moon sitting in Crescent car.

III.

Sweetheart, thy thought,
In the soul inwrought,
As sinks in gloom the red-orbed sun,
While out of the dark
The shimmering spark
Awaits to embrace the white faced moon.

IV.

Where crimson glows,
On the umber floes,
And hills are ablaze with saffron warm,
As Druid's blood,
In terraced wood,
The dun west scatters its magic charm.
The Dorian maid,
In the gathering shade,
With veil all yellow and silver beam,
Like elfin sprite,
Reflects a light,
Cold as the ice, or a vestal's dream,
The zephyrs sigh,
As the robes trail by,
Of sad-eyed night, in the pulseless main,
While belted Mars,
'Mid sentinel stars
His first watch keeps o'er the distant plain.
If seraphs be
On this sparkling sea,
And, fluttering, wing the weird expanse,
Does Love have birth
So far from earth,
And pierce the ether with his shining lance?

V.

Sweetheart, this land,
Where the fairies stand
On the velvet dale and peaceful shore,
With jeweled crests,
By the Genii's nests,*
Is the mystic spot of childhood's lore.
In frolic grace,
Through azure space,
The elves will tempt our vain desires;
As spectres grim,
Near forests dim,
Decoy to ruin with phantom fires.
On burnished steep,
As they vigils keep,
The crown'd Gnomes muster in helmet sheen;
But thy sweet smile,
Thy charms beguile
My sense from all this radiant scene.
'Twas witchcraft sips,
From ruby lips,
That Sappho's flaming verse inspired,
Falernian wine,
Pure love divine,
That Grecian, Roman heroes fired.

---

* See description in " Vathek," of the nests above the clouds, where
the good Genius placed the children rescued from the Giaour.

As yon dappled cloud,
With gray-rimm'd shroud,
Obscures the zenith in mantle gray,
By the girdled zone,
And melting tone
Of the foam-born queen of Paphos' wave,
O sweetheart rare,
This love we'll bear,
From tangled maze, o'er the surging tide,
Our now, ours then,
And still our when,
We thread the blue concave side by side.

BY THE MOUNTAIN AND THE SHORE.

WHERE the dreamy waters murmured,
　　Fleck'd with gold and amber hued,
'Midst the phantom shadows stealing,
　　From the copse of birchen wood;
Where the green waves, fondly dashing,
　　Beat the shore in circlets nigh,
Stood at eve a sparkling maiden,
　　Light her heart, and bright her eye.

Mute beside the glassy river,
　　Twilight shading wood and sky,
Here 'twere joy to live forever —
　　In the forests live and die;
Where the waves, each other chasing,
　　Bathe the sedge upon the shore,
Dwell upon this fairy margin
　　In the glen forevermore.

NOTE.—Written at the Glen House, White Mountains, for Miss Stella Beeson, July, 1882. The next morning our tourist party left for the sea shore. The references are to "Emerald Pool" and the river near Glen House. Mount Washington the monarch of the hills, and the four other highest peaks in the White Hills, face the Glen House.

"A penny for your thoughts," young tourist,
  Ere these magic scenes depart;
Shall regrets forever haunt thee,
  Dim the eye and cloud the heart?
Fairy glen and dancing river,
  Tangled path beside the shore,
Melt away from earthly vision,
  Memories, and nothing more.

Then her mouth with smiles was kindled,
  Laughter floated on the breeze,
As she coaxing called upon me,
  " Write some poetry, won't you, please?"
The evening wind was gently rustling
  Through the daisies wet with dew,
The yellow stars were dimly peeping
  O'er the mountain's crest of blue.

Shall I write a goblin story,
  Legend old with horrors fraught,
While the hoary mountains beckon
  Themes from out the world of thought?
Or, shall laughter fright the spectres,
  Wailing in the mournful pines,
And the echo of thy spirit
  Ring the measure of the lines?

Thou must leave the rippling waters
  Where the twilight trembling stays,
Emerald Pool and frowning mountains
  Be a thought of vanished days.
Yet will fancy sometimes linger
  On the mountains grim and hoar,
Formed by HIM who keepeth ever
  Watch and ward beside the shore.

Gilded hours are swiftly passing
  By the crystal hills and streams,
And our tourist rounds of pleasure
  Soon will be but idle dreams;
Still the elfin lamps will glitter
  On these purple rocks below,
Still the azure dome of heaven
  Will with starlight be aglow.

Radiant morning hence shall lead thee,
  And the night shall lull to sleep,
By rocky coast and beaches sandy,
  To the music of the deep.
May HE whose temples are the hills,
  Whose shrines are by the shore,
Watch o'er this wand'ring tourist fair,
  Where billows ceaseless roar.

Soon thou shalt see the red-orbed sun
    From ocean waters rise,
With flaming pennons floating far
    Athwart the eastern skies;
And mark the change to golden hue,
    As, springing from the waves,
The day-god drives his chariot
    From Neptune's coral caves.

And thou shalt see his lances gleam
    Far as the eye can reach,
As, tinged in foam, the white-caps break
    On Nahant's shell-girt beach.
And thou shalt see, when perfect day
    Is cloudless in the light,
The fair and distant sails go by,
    Like phantoms dim and white.

And thou shall stand where surging tides
    On rocks eternal beat,
And cast the treasures of the sea
    Beneath thy wandering feet ;
And strange and far these hills will be,
    Whose summits on us peer,
While near and clear the ocean's roar
    Is thundering in the ear.

Lake and river, glen and mountain,
  Ocean, cave, and tide-washed strand,
Forms of beauty, shapes of wonder,
  Fashioned by an all-wise hand,
Wheresoe'er thy fate may lead thee,
  Sheltered in His strong embrace,
May no blight of care or sorrow
  Darkly shadow thy young face.

And when other scenes and places
  Drive from thought this magic glen,
Keep this counsel traced sincerely,
  By a fellow-pilgrim's pen :
Keep, O keep, in wood or city,
  In the crowd, or when alone,
Keep, O keep thy joyous nature,
  'Tis a treasure, all thine own.

MIDNIGHT IN THE GLEN.

(INSCRIBED TO MY DAUGHTER NELLIE.)

Spirits with :

> —— "haunts in dale or piny mountain,
> Or forest by slow stream or pebbly spring,
> Or chasms and wat'ry depths.—"
> ——*The Piccolomini.*

I

At midnight, in a cloudless sky,
  The climbing moon uprose,
On sombre vales and glassy brooks
  Its mellow color throws;
Now resting in the lines of light,
  Now dancing o'er the rills,
Fantastic shapes and gleaming sprites
  Are flitting in the hills.

II

The bright-eyed deer, with graceful bound,
  Stop near the limpid streams
To gaze upon their beauty fair,
  Reflected by the beams.

By mountain trees that cluster o'er
  The tranquil, silent lake,
The wand'ring eagle furls his wings,
  While night-birds are awake.

III

The trout, swift swimming through the wave,
  Gay tenant of the stream,
Has plunged into its hidden depths,
  And vanished like a dream;
And now on couch of radiant shells,
  Forgets the coming day,
When from the wanton wave he leaps,
  The cruel angler's prey,
And all that breathed, or all that moved,
  Had sought their place of rest;
The night was calm, and still, and fair,
  In golden colors dressed.

IV

But hark! a swell of murmurs strange,
  From coverts in the hills,
Deep as an organ's volumed tone,
  The night-air slowly fills;

And now it rises, dirge-like note,
    Unto the cloudless blue,
The midnight song of mountain fays,
    And Gnomes of dusky hue;
For there are forest fairies here,
    Who from the caverned shades
Come forth and hold their revels loud,
    In lonely mountain glades.
Upon the snowy giant's crown,
    As hand in hand they go,
The phantom host in festal glee
    Leer down on us below.
They scowl at all that's innocent,
    Enchanters of the wood,
And try, by all the tempter's art,
    To overcome the good.
O step not in their magic ring,
    At midnight in the glen,
Or shining glamour fades away—
    Thou art the demons' then!
Hear not the mountain's clear cut chime,
    Nor listen to its moan,
Nor search its hidden rocks of gold,
    When night is on her throne.

V

But still the blue sky smiles above,
    So saintly and so fair,

And wild flowers whisper as they hear
  These voices of the air.
Soft voices charm to dreams unsought,
  In nature's temples then,
And in the valley all is peace,
  At midnight in the glen.
There is an eye, by day or night,
  Its vigils still will keep,
On mountain crest and valley lone,
  Where mortals weary sleep;
So thou but trust thine all to Him,
  And to His words be true,
Nor mountain sprite, nor midnight Gnome,
  Can harm bring unto you.

WHITE MOUNTAINS, July, 1882.

"LIKE TO A WATER COURSE."

LUCAN, SAT. IV., 182.

How gently all the days glide by;
   Like shadows come, in bubbles go;
The rippling hours pass quietly,
   Like to the streamlet's noiseless flow.

These are the careless days of youth,
   When ev'ry hour is glad and free;
The heart is fresh, and full of truth,
   Ere wrecked on Time's resistless sea.

The brook becomes a river soon,
   The child a man at length will grow;
His morning merges into noon,
   As waters gather in their flow.

The rill was clear—the larger stream
　　Is dark and turbid in its bed;
Such doth the face of boyhood seem,
　　And such when years roll o'er the head.

The river reaches ocean's tides,
　　Is lost in wand'ring in the wave,
And man, who on Time's surface rides,
　　Is soon forgotten in the grave.

DOUBT.

STILL doth the vital spark remain,
   Another Winter multiplies
The doubts, the hopes, the joy and pain
   Of years long past;
This troubled siege of vain surmise,
   Will it forever last?

Are there no certainties in view,
   Nothing to which the mind can cling?
Some sweet existence, sure and true;
   Something we feel,
To the fevered sense will bring,—
   An opiate to heal?

Or like yon dark and wintry sky,
   Despair its gloomy shadow flings
About the soul so blightingly,
   That hope expires:
All scorched the heart's most limpid springs,
   All quenched its brightest fires.

NOTE.—Written in Missouri.

Glorious spirit of this frame,
  Thou art not thus a slave;
Awake!—to bolder thoughts—for shame!
  Break through this chain
That makes thy traitor doubts thy grave,
  And be thyself again.

Beautiful is reason; but with Faith
  The weak clay radiates with light;
A glory strange will fill the brow,
  A lightning thrill
Pervade the frame, and gild the night
  With an electric will.

The fearful heart will melt in joy;
  Weakest, when, with a giant's might,
The very elements its toy,
  Are made—defied,
Again to damp the spirit bright,
  Once shrinking by their side.

Melt, O heart, in solemn prayer,
  And seek for courage firm on high;
Let Faith soar through the viewless air,
  Breathe the pure flame,
And drink in *that divinity*
  Earth can not give or tame.

"DREAMS HAVE THEIR DEVELOPMENT."

—Shelley.

ALONG Missouri's turbid stream
   The sunset fell,
With golden glow, in dying beam,
   That trembled fitful on the wave
With gentle swell,
   Or wandered into darksome cave.

Musing on the buried past,
   In reverie lost,
Among fading hues too bright to last,
   A stranger by the stream reclined,
By memory tossed,
   And the impulse of his former mind.

He dreamed of far-off days of song,
   When from each grove
Soft chastened music floated along
   On the balmiest Autumn air,
When life was love,
   And earth and morn were young and fair.

NOTE.—By Missouri River, 1858.

Airy and full of frolic grace,
  Lovely to sight,
Strangely beautiful in form and face,
  Ambition to his dreams appeared,
Seeming to invite
  Where now enchanting · melodies were
    heard.

Where sweetest fruit, blushing
  On the cool spray
Of most brilliant fountains, gushing
  Up from the green, grassy sod,
'Mid scenes ever gay,
  Where no labor swayed its rod.

Life has its fittest image here,
  As it should be;
Lovely and pleasing; no fear, no care;
  Poetic taste and sentiment,
From the gross flesh free,
  On hopeful youth and heart are blent.

While thus he dreamed, a cloud
  Came o'er the scene,
But hid not hearse, and pall and shroud,
  And saddened mourner close behind,
The same that, 'midst this green
  Calypso haunt, so charms the dreaming mind.

Ambition fades; toil shades his eyes;
  A mist was spread;
He saw work-shops, with amazed surprise,
  And toiling inmates, to whom day
Brought strife for bread,
  To whom *Duty* was Faith's brightest ray.

Faith indeed was there,
  A shape divine,
More beautiful with her lines of care,
  More happiness in her gentle smile,
Than all the speculations fine,
  And idle dreamings which the soul beguile.

The stranger saw a cheerful home,
  Gained by patient toil;
Then, urged by trust in better days to come,
  His dreaming ceased, and he began
To shake off the coil
  That bound him, and arose *a truer* MAN.

IMPROMPTUS.

THIS village is called a *model* place;
   May glory encircle its brow;
Its people are sadly *minus* in grace,
   Though troth they are *graceless* enow.

Blue and calm the gentle sky,
Softly bubble the waters by;
Heaven above us, heaven around us,
No art of man to cramp and bind us.
Far away all busy matters,
Far away the footstep patters;
Here, beneath the forest trees,
Let us take our quiet ease.

Living is a humbug,
   All of us know it;
Death is a blessing—
   "Pray, sir, show it."

What a de'il of a shame ;
Indeed, you're to blame,
That a man of your name —
So ancient a name —
Should foolishly throw away fame,
Should scornfully toss away fame,
And think it sublime,
And call it sublime,
To grab at a dime,
To catch at a dime,—
Like all the world catch at a dime,
Like all the world *die for a dime.*

How sadly rings the Autumn blast,
In mournful tones, that Summer's past;
The days have shortened, nights are dreary,
The falling leaves, like age, are weary ;
The sullen winds now rule the hour,
And teach us all grim Nature's power ;
All beauty fades and dies away,—
Type, O man, of thy sure decay.

GOLD.

Powers of beauty, charms of love,
Earth's gifts below and hopes above ;
Glory of wisdom, light of mind,
Fireside Lares, affections kind,
Must ye all bend to world's base law, —
That *cash* alone can give us *stamina!*
That court you must dame Fortune blind,
If aught of this world's sneer you mind.
Go seek for gold ; don't seek in vain,
But get your niche in marts of gain.
This gives you place, and magic name,
Where brokers dwell with gilded fame ;
Do this, or pass to shadowy grave
With broken hopes, which cannot save
Your toes from tread of rich and great ;
For this, alas! is poor man's fate.
So press on quick, break through the cloud,
And march along with Mammon's crowd ;
In hell you'll see the Gold-god's face,
And take, for aye, your destined place.

TO A YOUNG HUSBAND.

Constant shine the stars by night,
Calm and pure their holy light,
In the vaults of ebon sky,
When the evening shadows die.
See these emblems true above,
Perfect peace and perfect love;
Then hold thy bride near to thy heart,
Be true to her till life depart;
For *her* soul, in trust to thee,
More constant is than stars you see.
Richer than all earth's countless gems,
All thy love her true heart claims;
No fears has she, in faith divine
All *her* confidence is *thine*.　　.

ON THE SAME.

The mist was on the mountains,
　And the dew upon the thorn,
And sparkle in the grasses
　Upon our wedding morn.

The woman gave to me her life
  Without a murmuring word;
The mist gave way to sunshine
  As she spoke the fateful word.
A dirge to all old bachelors,
  A wreath for my lady gay;
A smile for the charming bridesmaids,
  A health to the wedding day.

TO MY CIGAR.

SWEETLY it curled through the evening air
   In wavy wreaths toward the azure sky,
   Gracefully twisting on high,
Suggesting visions bright and fair;
   A looming castle forms,
   Now clouds portending storms,
And then, Chameleon like, new shapes assumes,
'Till, tired, coquettish thing, its early hue
   resumes.

Heavenly art thou—Spanish cigar;
   Violets have no fragrance like to thine;
   By many a forest shrine,
Welcoming the evening star,
   The meditative thought,
   The absent loved ones brought,
To thee I owe, parent of a gentle creed,
Ethereal, dusky, Indian weed.

NOTE—An early rhyme for the press, in Clermont *Courier*, 1855.

Brilliant stars of the Summer night, ·
  Thy radiance falls on hill and stream;
  Oft by a transient beam,
'Neath crags revealing jewels bright,
  With a social cigar,
  I gaze at thee afar,—
Afar in the depths of the limitless blue,
Glorious types of the beautiful, holy and true.

Thou wondrous wise yet silent sage,
  My choicest friend through changing years,
  If ever shall come the cares,
The restless whims and griefs of age,
  Through thy smoke I can smile
  At the world and its guile,
And if fastened for aye in woman's sweet net,
THEE, O precious Havana, I cannot forget.

'TWAS ON A STARRY NIGHT.

'Twas on a starry night in June;
    The Summer then was in its pride,
And softly gleamed the silver moon
    Upon Ohio's rippling tide;
When through the forest dense I strolled,
    Nor gave a thought to objects near,
For *thou*, sweet lass, it must be told,
    Were to my fancy then most dear.

I thought but of your sparkling eyes,
    The raven tresses of your hair,
Where Cupid, watching, ready lies,
    The gazer's senses to ensnare.
Though time and care may bend me down,
    And troubles may my freshness sear,
Yet still my heart will always own
    That *thou* to me art ever dear.

Maysville, Ky., 1850.

Note—See poem "*Constancy*," on page 76, a sequel to this.

TO THE GIRL OF MY HEART.

Whilst the Earth, with sunset glory,
 Seems to mock the raptured eyes,
And from copse and silent water,
 Shadowy vapors slowly rise;
And the song of birds is fading,
 Like our early dreams of love,
I behold the starlight creeping,
 From the azure vault above.

The hour recalls old memories,
 Memories crowned in burnished gold;
And my heart is filled with gladness,
 As the sunlight fills the wold.
A spirit threads my lonely chamber,
 Spirit with an aspect bright,
Seems to be about me flitting
 While a mist enshrouds my sight.

Note.—On a Clermont County farm, 1855.

Why breathes the image words of sorrow,
　　Words of sorrow and of doubt?
Why does it change my joy to mourning
　　As the cypress waves without?
Whilst its dark eyes, rich with meaning,
　　Flash upon my musing mood,
Like a star might pierce the darkness
　　Of some ancient beechen wood.

Why this glance of sad inquiry?
　　Why this voice of softened tone?
Is thy grief forever banished,
　　And thy phantom doubts all gone?
Tell me, wilt thou, gentle beauty,
　　By the stars so mild and bright,
Crown me once again with gladness,
　　As the moon exalts the night?

Quell thy murmurs, lady charming,
　　Lull the storms within thy breast;
Like the ocean, calm and peaceful,
　　Gently sink thyself to rest.
Leave to me the gloomy cypress,
　　Let it all my pleasures mar;
Leave my soul on skyward pinion,
　　Soaring off to greet the star.

The spirit is an odorous flower,
   It but thrills by sweetness wild;
The stars in colored arch of heaven
   Suit but the whims of dreamy child;
Let both be types of hope and beauty,
   Which, like blending waves of sea,
Tremble through the heart's dim chambers,
   To at last unite in thee.

DO I THINK OF THEE?

O THOU bright and joyous maiden,
　By the sky above me bending,
　By the sky-lark's upward tending,
　By thy presence beauty lending,
　　I do think of thee !

Thou who hast my heart's devotion,
　By the rose with dew-drops shining,
　By the hedge that rose is twining,
By the clouds in airy motion,
　　I do think of thee!

Ah! these symbols ever fleeting,
　Not by them I would convey
　Thoughts which 'round thine image stray,
But by love's own pulses beating,
　　I do think of thee!

Lady, may the twilight kiss thee,
　And with lips of sweetest balm,
　In some hour of musing calm,
Whisper at even, how I miss thee,
　　How I think of thee.

IMPROMPTUS.

AFAR I see thee in this place,
I gaze upon thy dreamy face,
  And turn away and sigh;
My soul doth shrink as I gaze at thee,
For I know such beauty like the sea,
Coquettish scorns a man like me,
  Whose love shows *in his eye.*

Before the vision see a gorgeous scene,
A wide savanna of eternal green,
So far extended that its ocean hue
At length seems mingled with the sky's deep
  blue.

On the prairie.

In glittering car
  From out the purple East,
With pomp Apollo comes,
  Lord of the feast;

His golden sparkles
   Glisten in the streams;
The ancient woods
   Warm up to greet his beams;
The gurgling waters
   Foam in bubbles bright;
The Spring-clad verdure
   Glares upon the sight,
And the village wakes
   'Mid arrowy lines of light.

Sunrise.

Cloud in mantle dark and gray,
Hide from sight the garish day;
Let mellow tinges fill the hazy sky,
And calm and gently daylight die,
And while the charm is on each tree,
Wander, my heart, O love, to thee.

A FACT.

Two Clermont brothers, as the story goes,
Who married sisters, each had woes.
Each husband loved his brother's wife,
And then began an endless strife;
Which, to conclude, the neighbors tell,
They traded wives, and all went well.
They followed that old Roman, Cato,
(Though neither had, *perhaps*, read Plato)
Who, when his lady proved contentious,
Kindly loaned her to his friend, Hortensius.

O day of splendor,
　Day of life and glee,
Shine thou on all
　With joy, save me;
For I, with soul
　So bowed with care,
Envy the birds
　Whose pinions gleam in air,
And have no heart
　For aught that seems so fair.

In sickness.

Hazy, balmy, Indian Summer,
  Golden days of Autumn glory ;
Lazy, dreamy, rich October,
  Passing by 'mid sunsets gory;
Somber Winter, Winter sober,
  Sighing comes decayed and hoary,
Muse we all on splendors past,
Indian Summer cannot last.
Closing on us, harsh November,
  Leafless forests, woods forlorn,
Dreary weather; short days gloomy ;
  Sol the while in Capricorn.
Cheerful fires in places roomy,
  As we "double 'round the horn, "
Listening to the ancient liar,
In his seat by grocery fire,
Tell us all about hard Winters,
  All the wiles of politicians,
Wars and gossip, murders bloody,
  Who is sick, and what physicians;
Talk of lawyers, also preachers,
  Show the ways of sharp tacticians.
To listen, *we*, but *his* to talk,
He makes us all walk up to chalk.

.

Soft o'er the village the gray dawn is stealing,
   Tinging the landscape in beauty and grace;
Shadows are falling from house-top and ceiling,
   Shadows are resting on baby's sweet face.
Silently, gently, the darkness is shrinking,
New life the morning is eagerly drinking.
Lovingly stepping, Aurora comes sighing,
   Where the sweet baby is fading away ;
Hazy his forehead ; see, he is dying!
   Aurora has opened the gates of the day,
And clasping the spirit from dead baby riven,
Has left with the living a brief smile of heaven.

1876.

The Past, why should we e'er regret it ?
'Tis gone, so let us all forget it.

Heaven shield thee, heaven bless thee;
  Life be filled with happy hours;
Fortune guard thee, fortune watch thee;
  Fate strew thy path with flowers.
If I love thee, do not scorn me,
  Still my prayers are for your sake,
Thinking of thee; can't forget thee,
  Passing through life's giddy wake.

THE LUXEMBOURG.

(TO MY COUSIN, MRS. F. W. ARMSTRONG, PARIS, JULY 21, 1883.)

WE saw the Sculptor's art in stone,
 And cunning skill in bronze and gold :—
From painted canvas on us shone
 The Heroines of ages old.
The faultless form, the classic face,
 The soul which glows in passion there ;
The nameless charm, the high-born grace,
 Which makes each lady seem so fair.

The roses bloom, the fountains play.
 Serene and cold, in marble grand,
The Queens who ruled in by-gone day
 Illustrious on the Terrace stand,—
Marguerite de Provence, proud and fair,
 arguerite de Valois, false and vain ;
Marguerite Splendid, of Navarre,
 Marguerite of Anjou, doomed to pain.

NOTE—Mr. F. W. Armstrong was educated in Paris, and passed daily through the *Jardin de Luxembourg* to school in the Latin Quartier, to which allusion is made in the poem.—

The Troubadour their praises sung,
   The armored knight set lance at rest;
Great Princes on their accents hung,—
   To die for them was to be blest.
For them the tocsin called to war,
   The soldier lonely vigils kept;
The moon from sky, in Crescent car,
   Smiled on the spot where Beauty slept.

Where gleams the Lake in shadow *there*,
   A school-boy stooped his head to lave;
Or on yon seat, when free from care,
   He gazed at Tritons in the wave.
Where giant trees o'erspread the lawn,
   Saw *then*, as *now*, in regal state,
These marble Queens—that sculptured Faun,
   A Cupid *here* and *there* a Fate.

Beneath the same deep azure sky
   His path lay *here*—in boyish glee
To studies *then;* but *now* a tie
   Still stronger binds his life to thee!
With modest thought, and gentle creed,
   O study well each other's weal,
Which pulseless Hebes do not heed,
   Or stately Courtiers think or feel.

And turn from all these gems of Art,
　To husband, daughter, near and dear,
And kinsman's warm and friendly heart,
　Which envies not the splendor here.
For in these Gardens, once of Eld,
　This haughty Lord, *that* jewelled Dame,
Their gilded revels nightly held,
　While France lay reeking in its shame.

For thee a nobler lyric crown,
　It cannot deck a fairer brow;
May Time press lightly with his frown
　Where youth and sunshine cluster now.
And when is reached Eternal seas,
　And sullen tempest's moaning roar,
May HE, who calms the rising breeze,
　Guide thee and thine to Golden Shore.

In Highland Hills, in gladsome Spring,
　While bubbling waters soothe the ear,
At Winter eve will memory bring
　Again these scenes which linger here.
The sculptured forms in dreams will rise,
　This charming music make refrain;
These phantoms pass before the eyes, —
　The Luxembourg return again.

CONSTANCY.

HE wrote her name in all his books,
    And carved it on the trees;
He heard it in the murmuring brooks,
    And whispering in the breeze.
'Twas music in the mountain glades,
    In meadows green or brown;
By torrent's rush, in forest shades,
    In grassy lane or town.

At morning's blush, and evening's gloam,
    She held his sense in thrall;
At church, or ball, at school or home,
    She was his *all in all !*
He loved—or thought so;—so did she,
    And on Kentucky's shore
They pledged eternal constancy,
    To last forevermore !

NOTE—See lines. "' *Twas on a Starry Night*," in this book, on **page 62.**

They parted—'twas with tears and sighs,
   Like lovers who were older;
He kissed her forehead and her eyes,
   She—wept upon his shoulder.
When shall they meet? And how, and where?
   Can time their hearts dissever?
O no!—by Earth, and Sky, and Air,
   No!—never! never! never!

The years flew by—they met again,
   And did not know each other;
She tried to call his name in vain,
   He—thought she was her mother.
The angel of the school-boy's lays *
   Had lost her glory now;
No longer love's all-glowing rays
   Saw halos 'roun   her brow.

No raven tresses met the view,
   No braids in charming grace;
The hair was dyed—its dingy hue
   Was suited to the face
Where once had shone those lustrous gems
   So sparkling .with delight;
Green goggles, with their circled rims,
   Now met the gazer's sight.

* *"Tempora mutanter et nos mutamur in illis."* At 40.

Were they sad, or broken-hearted?
　Did they act the fool?
Talk of days so long departed,
　In novels that's the rule?
O no! but rather, *quantum suff*—
　Of weather, crops and oil,
Of Bourbon, mules, tobacco, snuff,
　Of blue-grass, and the soil;

And of her husband, who, 'twas said,
　Like Midas, king of old,
Though asses ears adorned his head.
　Had coffers lined with gold.
Again they parted—nothing more,
　The past was mentioned *never!*
Are these the same, who long before
　Had pledged their faith *forever?*

ABSENT.

Absent Ella, absent Ella,
  All alone art thou to-night;
All alone am I, dear Ella,
  By my study fire's red light.

Art thou lonely, gentle Ella,
  Lonely when away from me?
I am lonely, O *so* lonely;
  Should I not be when from thee?

I listen, for thy footsteps, Ella,
  Fall like music on the ear;
All is silent, save the echo,
  Whispering, "Ella is not here."

Shadows flit across my musings,
  Shadows spread along the floor;
Shadows full of memories
  Peer through my chamber door.

Something to my spirit utters,
  Ella weeps! she is in sorrow;
Is she weeping in her absence?
  I will fly to her to-morrow.

TO HER WHO UNDERSTANDS THEM.

Ah! toss that witching fairy head,
  No Zephyr from the bright blue sea,
With wilder joyance drops its curls
  Amidst the blossoms of the lea.
And turn again that swimming glance,
  And let me dream awhile of heaven,
The purple glory of the sky,
  The weird, wild star of even.

Ah! once again that love crowned smile,
  On Como's lake, the wave all bright,
With vernal hues and azure sheen,
  Does not shed forth such gladdening light.
And breathe again those magic words,
  That thrill the soul with choral song,
Those tones that waft the spirit by,
  Groves and choral halls among.

But why these whims of fond desire?
 No right have I to claim thy love ;
None but to gaze as at some bird,
 That soars in yon blue vault above.
But oft the bird to earth descends,
 And fills with vesper hymns the air;
Dear maiden, be to me that bird,
 And break this cloud of care.

In Clermont *Courier*, 1854.

AFTER MARRIAGE.

THE days of yore have joined the past,
    And buried are their smiles and tears,
While o'er my path new hopes have cast
    The light of brighter years.

I turn from those receding hours
    That now can charm no more;
They fade like withered Summer flowers,
    Whose witchery is o'er.

I cannot shed a single tear
    Upon my vanished dreams,
So brightly glows the coming year,
    Tingéd with the future's beams.

Too long ideal joys have shed
    O'er me their spectral light;
Into a truer life I'll tread,
    'Till Day wanes into Night.

Batavia, Ohio, 1857.

The rose is freshened by the dews
  Which shelter on its breast,
And *thou*, my wife, shalt be my muse,
  The latest and the best!

Farewell, ye shadows, and the song,
  That hovered o'er my way,
For other ties are still more strong,—
  Immutable as day.

Hail! hail! thou bright and lustrous morn,
  All cloudless still shall be
The future; let the past now go,
  Since Mary came with me.

For Mary's love is dearer far
  Than all I yet have won;
I sang it as the evening star,
  'Tis now to me the *Sun*.

IMPROMPTUS.

GOOD by, dull care,
I never share
My place with such as thee,
But ever dare
To live as rare,
As rare can ever be.

Come like shadows, so depart;
Thus I cast thee from my heart;
Go and hide thee, for 'tis past,
'Twas my *first* love, and my *last.*

At 18.

There is no joy in universal space,
'Mid the cold bright stars above,
Save when the watch of night is given
To the sweet planet of Love.

IN AN ALBUM.

The years roll by ; may I yet hope
   That memory will recall the past,
Though short our lives in narrow scope,
   These lines will keep unto the last.

Time and decay will blast our youth,
   May this remembrance linger yet,
How on this day we pledge our troth,
   In friendship's ties, to ne'er forget.

The page, you see, is blurred by ink,
   And blots have marred its surface wide;
'Tis like my faults : O do not think
   Of these, but of my brighter side.

Maysville, Ky.

WHEN THE ROSY CHEEK IS PALING.

When the rosy cheek is paling,
   And the bright flush ebbs away,
Autumn winds seem 'round me stealing,
   Autumn shadows 'round me stray.
Some strange apprehension thrills me,
   Like the murmur of a stream,
And I see thee sadly floating
   Midst the vapors of a dream.

But when swift thine eye is glancing,
   Like a wave in sunshine crowned,
And thine airy foot is dancing,
   Fawn-like o'er the grateful ground,
And thine eagle spirit revels
   In the glory of the earth,
And thy sweet voice scatters accents,
   Rich with music and with mirth,

Then my fancy spurns the phantoms,
　　Pointing to the dread unknown;
Soars with thee to golden castles,
　　In some far Elysian zone;
Then the world seems clothed in beauty,
　　Hope and love twine chaplets fair;
Youth enwreathes the brow with roses,
　　Jewels deck thine auburn hair.

In what mood shall I behold thee,
　　When the sunset melts afar,
And o'er Miami's hills outreaching,
　　Shines the bright Hesperian star?
Shall I hear thy drapery rustling,
　　Spirit-like in azure space,
Shedding thoughts of fairy gladness,
　　Images of frolic grace?

No! such unsubstantial fancies
　　Mock the soul's sky-yearning flight;
I would see thy dark eyes flashing
　　In their own aerial light;
Feel thy living hand, warm throbbing,
　　In my own's responsive grasp;
Know thyself in chasteness resting
　　Trustingly within my clasp.

This may seem, O modest maiden,
　Vision of forbidden things;
Let it be so; in the desert
　Gush up bright imagined springs;
If they fade in mirage glowing,
　Still your fancy holds them fair;
So I woo thy presence, lady,
　Through the breathings of the air.

Batavia, Ohio, in Clermont *Sun.*

THE MISANTHROPE.

"Homo sum, et humani, a me nil alienum puto."

—Terence.

I

SOLITARY 'mid all this stir of busy life ; alone,
He treads this pleasant earth a stranger to its joys
    unknown,
For him no woman's love, no friendly grasp of
    neighbor's hand,
No children's smiles, no mother's kiss—this wan-
    derer in the land;
No mourning tears by him are dried, no sorrow fills
    the breast
Where selfish misery holds its court, and soul is at
    unrest ;
When suffering lies along his path, he turns in sul-
    len pride,
And, like the Levite and the Priest, "he takes
    the other side."

II

Apart in gloomy state he walks, nor mingles with
his kind,
The road long pressed by human feet suits not his
morbid mind;
No play for him, no sports allure, earth is a desert
wild;
Man loves him not, as he hates man; O was he e'er
a child?
Or did great Nature, in his case, reverse her com-
mon rule,
And mark him with the brand of Cain—this solitary fool?
To dwell in desolation's halls, unknowing and
unknown,
Despising and despised, to walk his selfish path
alone.

III

O seek for pleasure in this life, as swiftly pass the
years,
Take interest in your fellow-men, their hopes, their
plans, their fears;
Read of the men whose monuments are builded in
the heart,
Their speculations, goodly schemes, where mankind
took a part.

In business, love, or politics, the golden moments
    fly,
The busy man finds beauty still in earth, in air, in
    sky;
Or if you choose in Fashion's throng, or churches'
    graver tone,
Go mingle with the human crowd who do not live
    alone.

IV

Why lingers here this Ishmaelite? what is his final
    goal;
And will he always be alone, this miserable soul?
And still contemn our pleasant world, when in the
    silent land
No tidal wave can cast him back upon this hated
    strand?
Will he regret, upon that shore, the traveler's final
    bourne?
No feeling heart upon this globe for him doth weep
    or mourn;
And will he, in Elysian fields, still wander all un-
    known,
'Mid multitudes of buried dead, still tread his path
    alone?

ON THE SHIP.

FAIR Julia, rosy as the dawn,
When dew is glistening on the lawn,
  And morning light is shed,
Has crossed the river's surging tide,
Papa and mamma by her side,
  And loving brother Fred.

Belgravia at her anchor lay,
And Julia's heart was blithe and gay
  As vessel's deck is pressed,
For when on Brooklyn's heights the sun
Shall cast the evening shadows dun,
  She'll be on ocean's crest.

To home a long and lingering glance,
Then *bon voyage* to sunny France
  At tap of steamer's bell.
There stands the Lady Mary, bright,
With father, mother in delight,
  And also Cousin Nell.

NOTE— Miss Julia Kellog, Brooklyn, N. Y., Miss Mary Armstrong and
Miss Nelly Collins, of Hillsboro, Ohio. The first night on the Atlantic
outside of Sandy Hook, June 16, 1883.

Fair Julia lived upon the sound
Which circles all Long Island ground,
   Across the Empire Bay;
And Lady Mary, Cousin Nell,
Where Highland Hills, and shady dell,
   In western sunset lay.

The night has hid the land from view,
And sky and ocean's mingled hue
   Surround the children three;
And rushing waves and curling foam
Now dash upon the iron home
   Upon the boundless sea.

And Lady Mary, Cousin Nell,
And Julia fair, on billows swell;
   The Lord will safely keep.
This watchful Eye, on sea or shore,
Is sentinel at danger's door,
   Where innocence doth sleep.

FROM MY STUDIES.

(CINCINNATI, 1852.)

COULD my heart unfold to thee,
  Dearest girl, how fondly now
It muses on thy loveliness,
    Those eyes of light, that matchless brow,
      That sweetest smile,
    That voice of rarest melody,
It could but tell how these beguile
  My soul from book's dull slavery.

'Twould seem delirium all,
  This fairy land, where the sky
Kisses the velvet dale and stream,
    Warbling along in harmony
      With the song
    Of birds in the foliage green,
Flinging its jewelled drops along,
    So fair, so bright, so sweet a scene.

_____

NOTE—In a letter to a pupil in Oakland Seminary.

Rare, illusive dream; 'tis fled,
  As fade the flowers of the Spring;
As fade the Dolphin's golden hues,
  And twilight's gentle whispering;
    The city jars
  And studies call the absent ear
From its converse with the silent stars,
  And yet, with all, *thou* still art here.

In books thy glance is eloquent;
  I read, but hear *alone* thy speech;
I see thy form;—thy ruby lips
  With witchcraft all my senses teach,
    But love divine.
  Law has no charms; 'tis uninspired,
It has no touch of Love's pure wine,
  The touch which has my senses fired.

"What is writ is writ." Forgive
  If aught displease. Be kind as fair;
The harp which tempts should not repel
  The wooing fingers of the air;
    So now adieu!
  'Tis done—and once again the jar
Drives me from happiness. Too true
  That all our sunlight smiles afar.

BY FARM HOUSE GATE.

By farm house gate, as day goes out,
   And shadows fall, of darkened night,
The mists arise from circling stream,
   And dim the scenic world in sight;
The heart is crushed with sullen chill,
Which baffles hope and darkens will.

To Maysville Hills my memory
   Wings its glorious, golden flight,
Where boyhood hopes and visions breathe
   To boyhood's soul, so glad and bright;
So 'mid the lone scene my lot is cast,
Gleams the sunlight of the buried past.

Save hoot of owl, and frog's deep note,
   And forest's moanings, naught is heard;
To Maysville home all thought is turned,
   And like some worn and weary bird,
With flagging wings and anxious eye,
I turn to home, and can but sigh.

Note—An early rhyme, 1852, on a farm.

For thou, Kentucky, to my dreams
  Art Beauty, Music, softest light ;
In all things fair ; a radiant spot,
  Where never came the gloomy night,
Whose dusky shadows flit along,
As now the path I trace in song.

In solitude the mind will still
  Preserve the tints of boyhood's sky,
The sky where magic dwelt, and love,
  As days and nights went gaily by ;
When sorrow hid in dismal cell,
Joy reigned alone, bid grief farewell.

The farm house gate looks o'er the stream,
  Which murmuring falls on listening ear ;
The night wind wooes the forest trees,
  Nor other sound is lingering near ;
  I pause, and o'er the scene so drear
Send winging back to boyhood home
My vows and love, 'neath Heaven's dome.

.

CARE.

Who cuts so deep?
Who cuts so strong?
Who cuts for aye and ever?
Who brings us grief?
Who brings us tears?
And leaves us *never, never?*

'Tis Care, my boy,
Care, the tyrant,
Ever cutting with his lash;
None escape him,
None delude him,
Sombre, silent, gay or rash.

INVOCATION.

LORD, eternal, uncreated and supreme,
   Thy creature here before thee bows,
And humbly, on his bended knees, invokes
   THY grace to aid his future vows.
Sinful and weak, irresolute and vain,
   Without THY help he cannot stand;
Guide him, instruct his wandering soul,
   Direct his course to the better land;
Teach him THY living truth, confirm his hope
   Of heaven, and of eternal day,
And by THY *light dispel the clouds*
   Produced by Reason's glimmering ray.

THE OLD LAWYER.

You stand upon the summit now,
 And look back on your fading years;
The wrinkles creep upon your brow,
 The heart is seared by grief and tears.

Your dreams were vain; remorseless Time
 Has driven truth beyond your view;
How little seems the law sublime,
 When fifty finds you poor and *blue*.

You see we are but dreamers all,
 The real facts we sternly meet;
Dispel the shams at Fancy's call,
 And all we fondly thought to greet.

Where is your wealth, where is your fame,
 Where all your hopes of happy life?
Have you received more praise or blame
 In thirty years of Court-House strife?

A TOAST.

Come, fill me a cup,
Come, fill me a can,
We'll drink success to the Law:
Long may it flourish,
Long may it nourish
Men of small brains and of Jaw;
Come, jingle your glasses,
Toast all legal asses,
And those on whom is their Paw.

DON'T GIVE UP!

LET not, O friend, your courage fail,
  Or phantoms e'er beguile;
Let not your spirit basely quail
  If fortune doth not smile.

You see that man, so old and worn,
  His warfare nearly o'er?
All luckless has his life-work been,
  And troubles crowd him sore.

Dame Fortune sometimes, fickle jade,
  Turned him a smiling face,
But soon the gleams in darkness fade,
  And sorrow filled their place.

But what is life, that he should care
  How hard its trials be?
With all his fellow-worms he'll share
  Our mortal destiny.

SLANDER.

WHAT matters it, my dear young friend,
  What all these tattlers say?
They spend their time in gossip foul,
  By night as well as day.
To them each venomed word is sweet,
  Such poison is their food;
How dear to all their craven souls
  The slander of the good.

Beware of all such vermin vile,
  Nor give them any room
To use your name, or quote your words,
  Else you have sealed your doom.
From mouth to mouth the biting speech
  Of slander circles 'round;
All virtue's crushed, all honor's gone
  And grovels on the ground.

From idle tongues and wicked hearts
　　May you be ever free,
And ne'er to you such sorrow bring
　　As they have caused to me.
Always in life act well your part,
　　By duty only led;
Despise the gall this snaky gang
　　Will shower on your head.

Upborne by what you know is true, ·
　　Shun all the shallow fools
Who stir up mischief, unaware
　　They are but other's tools.
Thus may it be with you and me,
　　To act but for the right;
Let reason guide, leave gossip free
　·　To poison day and night.

UNDINE.

THE snow is white upon the plain,
  And flecked the turbid river;
The storm is rattling 'gainst the pane
  From mountain's icy quiver.

On Clermont streams and gentle rills,
  The time you well remember,
The white snow, on Ohio hills,
  Lay in the bleak December

The happy years too soon have fled,
  Since on that night, so lucky,
The path in snow unto *thee* led
  The lover from Kentucky.

'Twas at a ball, by country side;
  How sweet the country lasses,
How trim the rustic beaux in pride,
  As gazing in the glasses.

O, then you were a belle, you know,
  And danced with such perfection;
The rustic hearts were bowed in woe
  When gazing your direction.

Kentucky's humble Chevalier,
  Most humble in devotion,
To find to all you were so dear,
  Took then a serious notion.

He saw the witless rural youth,
  In idle jest and gaping,
Throng 'round the lass so pure in truth,
  And heard their vacant laughing.

So, 'neath an alcove's curtained shade,
  With heart in tumult throbbing,
Kentucky gazed on Clermont maid,
  And watched the monkeys' bobbing.

Now rustling like an Undine thou,
  In auburn curls and tarleton,
My heart was in my mouth, I vow,
  By manes of Sir Guy Carleton.

'Round swarm the verdant country clowns,
  Like moths about a candle;
They buzz despite fair Undine's frowns,
  Her curls they almost handle.

Poor fools, you simply singe your wings,
  Your wooing is unlucky;
Fair Undine all her treasure flings
  To lover from Kentucky.

So 'neath the lamp light's fitful gleam,
  Close by the " Beautiful River,"
We launched our life-boats in the stream,
  To float along together.

While our boat rides o'er the Rapid's swell,
  Where breakers rude are straining,
We dream we hear the wedding bell;
  Our hearts have no complaining.

O Undine mine, alive or dead,
  How, through all earth's hard leaven,
We see our worldly love must lead
  Our thoughts alike to heaven.

I look into my Undine's eyes,
  I learned to love so young and fair;
I find her heart is free from sighs,
  There is no shadow there.

The hurtling shafts of Fate remove,
  And harmless pass the eyes,
For Undine, in all trials, proves
  An angel in disguise.

Missouri, December, 1861.

THIRTY YEARS AGO.

TIME floods the mind with chequered scenes,
　　The current bears us on, but yet
There lingers, 'mid the buried past,
　　Some memories we can ne'er forget.
These memories beam with light afar,
　　And as the brook, the palm-tree's smile,
To pilgrim's eye on desert's sand
　　Their beauty doth the soul beguile,
　　Ah! is it *Mirage* all the while?

Shall hope as in that pilgrim fade,
　　When verdant slope and crystal stream,
And song and shapes of light float from
　　The landscape like some fitful dream?
If so, still clasp the fond deceit,
　　And cherish as a brighter thing,
Than reason calls from sober thought,
　　However rich and blossoming.

But no! these memories are no spell,
　　To lure the heart from truth away;
The plant that glistening scatters bloom,
　　Encurtained by the diamond spray,
Does not with livelier freshness cast
　　Its bloom on sky and earth below
Than we with eager senses dream;
　　We live the same as years ago.

1884.

THE ABBEY OF SAINT DENIS.

(FRANCE.)

HERE lie the kings of ages past,
　'Neath this old Abbey's Fane;
In shapeless heap their bones are cast,
　Like war's unburied slain.
Here *once* their plumes in triumph waved
　In bright and fair array;
Nought *now* but names, on tablets graved,
　But kings! O where are they?

The morning mist is floating o'er
　This strangest spot in France,
The shoes of wood now pace the floor
　Where rattled shield and lance;
From Dagobert and Charlemagne,
　To Bourbon's awful fate,
They sleep, these kings, no grief or pain,
　In dreamless silent state.

NOTE—Visited on a Sunday in August, 1883.

The centuries have darkly passed,
  So boundless in their sway,
Since Charlemagne's shrill trumpet blast
  Made listening slaves obey.
The conquering chief his helmet doffs,
  The brandished sceptre falls,
And silence reigns where vassal shouts
  Rang through the festal halls.

O curtained Past! O mystic Past!
  How weird this place appears,
Where sculptured kings, in marble cast,
  Recall the vanished years.
The dim Church flame in mockery throws
  Its light on hopeless gloom,
A taper's faint and flickering ray
  On every kingly tomb.

From Clovis fierce to Louis grand,
  The Dead are here inurned,
Each slumbrous form with folded hand
  And face to heaven turned.
Beneath these vaults, and Abbey dome,
  Immortal spirits throng;
Wild Fancy here can make its home,
  And Poets weave their song.

Unrolled the Ages spectral fly
   With boding raven's wing;
The clustering shades, in moaning sigh,
   Around our footsteps cling.
Cathedral lone, hold fast your gloom
   Where kings in slumber lie;
Let all who wish muse on the Tomb,
   Give me the sunlit sky.

GOOD BY.

I

Good by to the Island,
  Green Erin, good by :
To the mists on Killarney,
  The blue in thy sky,
To inlets and havens,
  The rocks on thy coast;
Thy true-hearted people,
  Of nations the boast.

II

Good by to Cork harbor,
  Where navies may ride
When storms stir the ocean
  In anger and pride.
As fogs gather 'round us,
  'Mid tempest's harsh roar,
As ship leaves the offing,
  My heart is on shore.

NOTE—Written in Queenstown harbor. August 27 1883, for some em-
igrants going to America.

III

And faith is unshaken,
  That yet the red hand
Of Vengeance will loosen
  The chains from the land.
O where is the siren
  With Liberty's smile?
O why has she slighted
  This sea-circled isle?

IV

O sleeping or waking,
  Wherever thou art,
The tears that are flowing
  Appeal to thy heart.
May Freedom then hasten
  The treasure to save,
And Erin will trample
  On Tyranny's grave.

V

The signal is given,
  The flag at the mast,
The farewells are spoken, —
  With many the last!

The ship has weighed anchor,
   The soul breathes a sigh;
In sorrow and silence,
   O Erin, good by !

THE HIGHLAND HILLS.

FAIR glows the morn on Highland Hills,
  How glad the sunshine beams!
How green the slopes in Summer dress,
  By Highland's pleasant streams!
Why stay so long by household gate,
  The parting word to speak?
What means this fullness of the heart,
  This dampness on the cheek?

'Tis done!   Farewell to wife and home;
  Regrets are now in vain;
Let memory have her perfect work,
  O'er mind, and heart and brain.
Farewell, the rock-ribbed Highland Hills,
  Each stream, and field and tree,
Nor still forget this Highland home,
  When far away at sea!

NOTE—On starting for Europe, June 11, 1883.

When fading hues of native shore
  Pass from the lingering sight,
And, round are swirling ocean waves,
  In mid-Atlantic's night;
When language strange and customs rude
  Assail the eye and ear,
Turn in the silent realms of thought
  To Highland Hills so dear.

Know ye beneath those craggy hills,
  And on their sunny slopes,
Are family, friends and household gods,
  And all your *earthly* hopes.
Nor time, nor tide, nor lands, nor seas,
  · *Nor foreign cities grand,*
Can dim the love of Highland Home,
  Where hills of Highland stand.

THE EMERALD ISLE.

We sailed around this sea-girt isle
  One Summer afternoon;
The ocean seemed on us to smile,
  That happy day in June.

And all is silent 'neath the sky,
  Nor sound of voices there,
But white-gull's shrill and piping cry
  Upon the ocean air.

Can we forget this lovely day,
  This green and rugged shore,
When first we saw the Irish Land,
  Then part to meet no more?

Can time or tide or poet's lay,
  Or seas which on us smile,
Make each or all forget this day
  We coast the Emerald Isle?

Note—Written on Anchor Line Steamship, "Belgravia," while steaming up St. George's channel, July 6, 1883.

How fair our skies, how bright the sun,
  This golden Summer day,
With Hope's firm "Anchor" at her prow,
  "Belgravia" rides the bay.

O! Faith's firm "Anchor," emblem fit
  To brace the mourning heart;
May every soul on this proud ship
  From this faith never part.

The gilded hours went swiftly by
  As o'er Atlantic tides,
'Mid music, song, and spirits light,
  Our vessel safely glides.

Now fair the seas, and short the hours,
  'Till landed at our port;
.We are at home in Irish waves,
  When anchor's penants float.

We see the verdured Irish coast,
  And Albion's haughty strand;
Do not forget *our home* at sea,
  When anchored on the land.

Soon we must part: O where to wander,
  Where to meet, ah! who can tell?
Are you ready for the summons?
  Can you tell us "all is well?"

Green will be this charming island,
   When thou and I, and all are gone,
And the ocean still forever
   Sing its mournful monotone.

The seaweed still shall drift in foam,
   And Dolphins change their hue,
And Nautilus spread its purple sail
   'Mid waters green and blue.

And other eyes shall idly gaze
   Where sky and ocean meet,
While 'round them spreads the wide, wide sea,
   A good ship 'neath their feet.

Farewell to Red-Cross flag at mast,
   Our emblem day by day;
On English soil we still will think
   Of our sailing up the bay.

ERIN.

(AS REPRESENTED IN ART.)

WHO is she now gazing
　　Across the dark sea,
With girdle unloosened,
　　And hair flowing free?
With hand on her forehead,
　　And feet in the wave,
Ariadne or Erin,
　　Can she be a slave?

The light-house is gleaming
　　'Mid shoals on the shore,
The ship is now dashing
　　'Mid breakers' dull roar.
O why does she linger?
　　How long shall she wait?
O tell us, dear Echo,
　　What shall be her fate?

NOTE—Stanzas for music. Liverpool, Eng., July 7, 1883.

The sad years are passing,
  Her face has grown pale,
With traces of sorrow,
  O will her hope fail?
As gazing, still gazing,
  Where sun sinks to rest,
For the true Prince in armor,
  From out of the west.

ALONG THE BOULEVARD.

I STROLLED, a stranger, on a Summer night,
Along the Boulevard, with its lines of light
And glamour gleaming on this fairy land,
With gilded phantoms gliding hand in hand,
From shining depths to far horizon blue.
No darkness here, but such a radiance, fair
As July suns, flood mid-noon's Gallic air;
The shadows creep and hide in dismal courts,
And leave the Boulevard to its festive sports.
These revelers see no pall or gloomy shroud,
But gaily prattle in the thronging crowd.
They hear no distant booming of the bell,
With sullen tone from vestibule of Hell.
With *no* belief, these creatures of a day,
When life is o'er, return again to clay.
Death ends it all, and so they pass along,
Enwreathed in pleasure, wine and song.
Here all is magic, and the flashing eye
Sees not that all this gaudy life must die.
No ear is turned to where sad labor groans,
And no heart throbs at misery's feeble moans;

NOTE—From Eglise Madeleine, to Colonne de Juillet, erected on spot
where the Bastille stood.   This is the oldest of the Paris Boulevards.

No voice is heard to cast a warning chill,
Bid pleasure cease and signal future ill,
For these "are to the manner born," while we
Live in a far-off land beyond the sea.
As strangers we may muse, and idly gaze
At novel sights in wonder and amaze;
As strangers join these "mummers" face to face,
And learn by practice all their ease and grace.
These smiles are false, and but an actor's part,
They charm the sense, but leave untouched the
      heart.
You look in vain for something good or true,
And do at last as all the others do.
Beware lest tempters in their nets enthrall
A soul forgetful of its duty's call.
'Tis three A. M., and waiting morn now peers
O'er the gay capital, which idly jeers
And still carouses with a ceaseless din,—
An earthly Pandemonium of sin.
The dashing Voiture with its coursers fleet,
And jewelled Houris flits along the street;
And coaches rattle 'mid the dazzling sheen
Of radiant vistas in the foliage green.
Through glowing panes shine wondrous works of
      art,
The spell of beauty to a tourist's heart.
'Neath arches, where the Sculptures nobly trace
Triumphant trophies of a by-gone race;

By Columns on whose storied summits stand
The heroes who have glorified the land;
By Cafes, where many a table bright
Jingles with glasses through the waning night;
By Ancient Gates we pass in dreams along,
And passages filled with mirth and song,
Where fair are all things, and how glad and free
Seem those who mingle in these scenes of glee.
Do these Blue-Blouses, flitting here and there,
Who seem in all this phantom life to share,
Deep in their souls have keen desire to slay?
And do they wander here in search of prey?
Are victims marked by Fauborg, Saint Antoine,
When Blouse shall rise to claim again his own?
When from alleys dark, and dismal den,
Shall surge a murderous mob of starving men!
Is there beneath this pageant's hollow show
Volcanic fires which in their embers glow?
Will Commune dread o'er Paris once more rise,
With terror burning in its lurid eyes?
Shall Columns fall 'neath desolation's tread,
And Palaces crumble with their weight of dead?
While fire shall waste these avenues and stalk
Resistless through each pleasant Summer walk,
Shall strangers search 'mid ruins. grim and bare,
For Eglise Madeleine with its saintly air,
Or Arc de Triomphe, Obelisk, or Fane
Of Notre Dame, and find their search in vain?

'Mid wreck of Revolution's ghastly shroud,
Which broods o'er Paris in a sullen cloud,
Will aught remain, except where proudly stands
The July Column, reared by Freedom's hands?
Whose sandaled Hermes overlooks the place
Where fell the Bastille in its deep disgrace;
'Tis on this spot, the despot's gloomy grave,
No Frenchman feels he e'er can be a slave.
Here ends our stroll, while Nemesis is dead,
And all the maskers nothing yet may dread;
To them all vows are false, all virtue lost,
And man upon a hopeless current tossed;
They know not home, nor kith, nor kind, nor kin
Amid this tapestry of gilded sin.
We, strolling strangers, lookers-on, alone,
Have something solid we may call our own,
And turn in gladness to the western sun,
In coming twilight when its course is run;
We see it sink to rest, and evening star
Stands trembling o'er a wave-washed land afar;
We think not, care not, for the ocean foam,
As thoughts go rushing to our far-off home.

Paris, France, July, 1883.

THE LITTLE CHILDREN.

PLAY on, dear children, have your fun,
   Take pleasure while you may;
No spots appear upon your sun,
   No clouds obscure your day.
Your cheeks, like roses, blushing red,
   Life has for you no thorn;
Then play till time to go to bed,
   And play again at morn.

The years will stay those little feet
   Which now so blithely run;
And footsteps lag upon the street
   When weary day is done.
Those little hands will rougher grow,
   That now can only play,
And trouble, then, the heart will know
   Where all is now so gay.

NOTE—It will be seen that the writer takes no stock in the maxim often spoken, that "children should be seen, not heard."

Those pretty eyes will lose their light,
    The voice will change its tone,
The tropic tints, which fill your sight,
    Will fade in frigid zone.
Play on, play on, this charming earth
    Is made for such as you;
For you its beauty, joy and mirth,
    Its gleams of sunny hue.

Play on, play on, and do not mind
    What cross old grannies say;
Such people should be deaf and blind,
    Play on, dear children, play.
Play on, play on, for night will soon
    Its sullen sceptre sway,
And evening close on childhood's noon,
    Play on, play on, to-day.

To-morrow there will quiet reign,
    Enthroned in silence, where
This childish music makes refrain,
    This laughter fills the air.
To-morrow desolation's gloom
    Broods o'er the empty hall,
No pattering footsteps in the room,
    No children's voices call.

To-morrow—mute the little lips,
    And still the restless feet;
The little hands with marble tips
    On pulseless bosom meet.
O where is then the noisy glee,
    The children's merry play,
The joyous romping, glad and free?—
    Let children play to-day!

My hair is gray; the years have set
    Their signet on my brow,
But must I in old age forget
    The little children now?
'Tis true I cannot jump and run,
    December is not May;
Don't mind me, children, have your fun;
    Dear children, play to-day.

Play on, play on, for time is brief
    To you, which seems so long;
And coming age, the wrinkled thief,
    Will hush your childish song.
Life is a game where cheats abound,
    And falsehood wins the day;
In childhood trust and truth are found—
    Let children play to-day!

April 12, 1884.

ON DUBLIN QUAY.

Slow sauntering with a friend, one day,
Along the lines of Dublin Quay,
The Red Cross flag waved in the light,
And Red Coat troops were in our sight;
Then Dennis spoke, but with a sigh,
With burning cheek and flashing eye:
"You see from every mast that flag;
Each fortress floats the hated rag,
Emblem of England's might and wrong.
We, silent, suffer, yet we long
The yoke to spurn from Celtic neck,
Which drags us at the despot's beck.
Can it be thought in us a crime,
The wish to rule our native clime?
Shake the long centuries' galling chain,
And be the lords of our own domain?
Must patriots hide in caverned glades,
Or lie in wait in forest shades?
Or anxious o'er the bounding wave
Await *thy* help the land to save?

You wonder why, in Phœnix Park,
Grim murder struck a shining mark;
Why, year by year, and day by day,
In Irish land is constant fray,
And o'er this crushed and bleeding isle
Assassination seems to smile.
See *that* Saxon's insulting tread,
He spurns the land of Celtic dead;
On all he fastens iron yoke,
These murders doth himself provoke.
Plunders the poor, this haughty snob,
Who only lives that he may rob;
He plants on us a hireling crew
Of thieves, and to exact their due
From peasant takes his hard-earned food,—
His cow, his pig, his poor abode;
Controls the purse, the sword, the trade,
The church, the lands, and has betrayed
To death this Naiad of the sea.
The soil, destined for brave and free,
This priceless jewel in Nature's crown,
In dust and scorn treads rudely down."
'Twas thus, while walking Dublin Quay,
That Dennis spoke to me that day.

August 24, 1883.

ESTHER.

Upon the mimic stage, in golden sheen,
    Ahasuerus, in his robes of state,
And gentle Esther, beauteous Queen,
    With Mordecai weeping at the Persian gate;
And Haman, haughty in his pride of place,
    And charming Zeresh, with her jewelled brow,
And the veiled Prophetess with native grace,
    Rebukes the harsh Median's cruel vow.
We hear the chorus echo to the sky,
    The praise of Haman, and the favored few,
So soon to hang full fifty cubits high
    On gallows built for Mordecai the Jew.
Ponder the moral here: the proud should learn,
    When they crush the lowly with their bitter
        frown,
That in the game of life the tables turn;
    The poor rise up, the haughty tumble down.

Note—Suggested on seeing the Oratorio by Hillsboro amateurs.

May all who scorn the humble peasant's lot,
   And in their wealth swell with inflated pride,
Remember that there is *one* equal spot
   Where wealth and poverty lie side by side.
Perhaps another when in death they meet,
   And all shall stand before "The Great White
      Throne,"
The Judge of all will strike the "balance sheet,"
   And 'neath the garb will recognize his own.
As gentle Esther for her race did sue,
   And found *them* favor in their greatest need,
So the Madonna, if the legend's true,
   Doth for the humble ever intercede.
Apparel, though with glittering jewels set,
   And earthly pride, and wisdom's high disdain,
And kingly crown, and ducal coronet,
   Are reckoned *dross*, and pleaded there in vain.
Such pleas are "sham," and when the "issue's"
      made,
   They win who *here* have had the purest hearts;
Though upstart greatness kept them in the shade,
   'Tis found at last they chose the better parts.

ENGLAND.

"THE people are but boorish masses,
Their lordship's humble, patient asses,
Whose cry is for queen, and church and State,
For 'jukes,' and 'earls' and Derby the Great;
Eat beefsteak rare; drink 'Hinglish Hale,'
And damn us Yankees 'till their glasses fail;
Pledge Wales' Prince, the kingly rake,
And love him for his mother's sake.
Even though a drunkard and a cur,
A prince, in 'Bull,' will find a worshipper;
For Bull is loyal, loyal to the core:
He loves a king, but loves his stomach more.
Fill him up with 'hash,' he'll never wince
At all the actions of the prince;
He fleeces strangers, lives by 'tips;'
Even his women take their 'nips.'
Bar-maids deal out the 'hale' and gin,
And deftly scoop the pennies in,
While beggars on the corner stand
And reach to all the out-stretched hand.

You pay for all you see or use,
No one will pounds or pence refuse;
In all your talk with great or small,
You find the *'shilling'* is 'all in all.'
The gush of Boston's traveled fools,
And all who are but England's tools,
Must not deceive, for this is true,
England's no place for me or you."
'Twas thus in Paris, near the Bourse,
A friend to me did hold discourse;
As I agreed with all he said,
I place it where it may be read.

COMING HOME.

I

THE headlands have vanished,
   No beacons in sight,
O'er wide wasting billows
   We plunge into night.
The wind, how it mutters
   And dashes the foam!
So farewell to Europe,
   The West is our home.

II

The ocean is sullen,
   The mad waves are high,
The lightning is gleaming
   Athwart the black sky;
We care not and fear not,
   And calmly can rest,
While proudly the good ship
   Sails into the West.

NOTE—On steamship "Illinois," September 5, 1883.

III

And welcome each morrow,
   Though fog may prevail;
Let billows surround us
   And fierce blow the gale,
Each gloom darkened even
   Has marked on the chart
The leagues we have measured
   To home of the heart.

IV

And nearer, still nearer,
   'Till bathed in the light,
The star-spangled emblem
   Is flashed on the sight.
One moment we linger,
   The Tender has come;
Farewell to the ocean,
   And welcome our home.

INUENDO.

DID you see that sneer?
It spoke a puppy's small soul slighted,
Whose shallow hopes the lady blighted,
    Now passing near.

A poisoned smile
Suggesting *that*, he dare not speak,
But leaves a meaning which you seek;—
    The lady's vile.

A scoundrel's leer,
Which seems to say, as she passed along,
In this craven mode of hinting wrong,
    She is not pure.

He thinks it scorn;—
'Tis but a coward's sneaking ire,
While envy burns his soul with fire,
    Of malice born.

A hint, a breath,
Insinuating *that* or *this*,—
With venom of a serpent's hiss,
    Producing death.

A point, a sign,
A meaning shrug, a hint obscure,
To sully those whom God made pure,—
    The sex divine.

This human crow
Looks not like eagle to the sky,
But turns to earth with leering eye,
    For something low.

A vampire foul,
A carrion ghoul, a social spot,
A crawling, creeping, wretched blot,—
    Base slander's tool.

The voice is hushed,
But in the look pollution lies;
'Gainst virtue every feature cries,
    And it is crushed!

A blur, a stain
On mother, daughter, wife and sister;
May all in Hades scorch and blister
    Who give such pain.

VALEDICTORY.

How many thoughts are dotted here,
　　Engraven on the silent page,
Catching each wayward hope and fear
　　Which mark the path from Youth to Age?

I soon to earth must say farewell!—
　　Perhaps in distant, future days,
　　When the dull ear is deaf to praise,
The scribblings of my youth forgot,
　　Thou able art at least to tell
　　How long ago a heart did dwell
　　Which found in thee a heart to speak;
　　The aims it missed, so sad and bleak,
For lingering years, *its joyless lot.*

What feelings cheer the gloomy way,
　　And 'rouse our better thoughts to start,
And cause our *ennuied* minds to stray,
　　But the *Faith* that strengthens every heart?

NOTE.

Dates are appended to many of the verses for obvious reasons, that those prompted by the gush and fervor of youth might be contrasted with the productions of maturer years. These selections were difficult to make in an accumulation of rubbish. Those made may not be the best, and after all, should perhaps have been consigned to the flames, as well as so many others, despite the verdict of partial critics whose judgment could hardly be deemed unbiased.

The earliest poem is "'Twas on a Starry Night," the latest is "Thirty Years Ago."

ADDENDA.

THE BOARD BILL.

(By Judge George B. Gardner, an impromptu at
court house table.)

The plaintiff must sue,
Her money was due;
By coaxing she got not a dollar.
Defendant did taunt
His old maiden aunt
Until she got "hot in the collar."

Defendant will claim,
Very much to his shame,
That aunty must pay for her *"ration,"*
Although it is shown
By every one known,
She came by his own *invitation.*

She worked every day,
"All work and no play,"
In sewing, in mending and sweeping.
Her money he got,
And always forgot
To pay, in spite of her weeping.

Note—The "old gal" got a verdict. On a second trial she got another verdict, and defendant "whacked up."

One stalwart Bushcreeker,
Quite fond of his liquor,
Used to get his old aunty to hide it;
When she told it in court,   ·
The lad's feelings were hurt,
And the rascal came in and denied it.

And Tom, a great strapper,
Would take aunty's napper,
If the law would but give him permission;
But at least her old back
. He would like for to rack
O'er the wash tub, without intermission.

And aye, the lad's father
Would very much rather
Make aunty an ancient street sweep,
Than let her raise honey,
And live on her money,
Which aunty so much wished to keep.

He forgot all the favors
And many endeavors
Of aunty to make them all happy,
And joined in a rout
To beat the "gal" out
Of the means she got from her "pappy."

So aunty, they said,
Was a pesky old maid,
With her "moughts" and her "moughtents"
    outrageous;
And must pay for her board,
While they kept her hoard,
But *nary a cent* for her wages.

TONY REPLIES.

Now you who saw that "board bill" rhyme,
  Come, hear the other side;
And when you've taken time enough,
  Perhaps you may decide.

In Summer and in Winter,
  In Autumn and in Spring,
For ten good years old aunty lived,
  And paid in promising.

A horse to ride and food to eat,
  A room kept nice and clean;
A doctor when she was not well,—
  In nothing treated mean.

She did no work and lived at ease,
  And claimed she paid her way;
But when she left she *sued* her host,
  Forgot her board to pay.

Ingratitude, those traitor arms,
  O'erthrew her kindest friend,
And aunty was bereft of charms
  When Court she did attend.

Her ten years' board she got for nought,
  'Twas that much saved by law;
But this sad lesson all may learn,—
  Don't trust an "old maid's" jaw.

They'll beat you, certain, "hit or miss,"
  No "odds" how sure your case may be;
If on this point you have a doubt,
  Board one ten years, and then you'll see.

WHAT "TOM" SAYS.

THERE was an "old maid,"
She threw in the shade
All chances our bill "for" to get;
No board was e'er paid
By "aunty," so staid,
The total sum due us, as yet.

Nobody would keep her,
This consummate weeper,
She wandered from "pillar to post;"
Not even a sweeper,
A cook or a reaper;
For *nothing* she lived on her host.

With plenty of money,
And two stands of honey,
She came with her "daddy," one day,
On a little black pony,
To see her friend Tony,
And bargain the price of her stay.

For seven long years,
'Mid sickness and tears,
She lived on the fat of the land,
Without any fears,
Regardless of jeers—
To work she ne'er raised a hand.

She would never pay board
While her cash she could hoard,
Or loan at high interest nappy,
Though given her word
It would all go toward
The payments of keeping her happy.

Take warning, my friend,
And don't horses lend,
Or keep open house for "old maids, "
Whose backs will not bend,
Who clothes will not mend,
And whose Board *will never be paid*.

NOTE—Upon reading the three foregoing squibs, my friend, Col. T. A. Walker, of Hillsboro, O., handed me the following *Impromptu* as an *addenda:*

BLOOD UPON THE MOON.

(BY T. A. WALKER.)

WHEN old Winter's blasts are over,
    And the Spring is drawing nigh,
We are pleased, in fact, "in clover,"
    'Neath the blue and softening sky.
While we discern from where we're hin'gin,
    In the morn, at night and noon,
That there's paint upon the Indian,
    And there's blood upon the moon.

We like conflict, or not danger,
    "In the bivouac of life;"
Like the warrior or the granger,
    Can conform to peace or strife.
So, farewell, home, our lovely Bingen;
    To thee return we may not soon,
For there's paint upon the Indian,
    And there's blood upon the moon.

In this conflict, as it fought is,
  Surely 'tween the right and wrong,
Help! O powers of light and darkness,
  Help, O! help the right along.
May not the strong on weak infringin',
  Mar the right or spoil the tune,
While there's paint upon the Indian,
  And there's blood upon the moon.

And whene'er the conflict's ended,
  And the flag of truce unfurled,
May a shout of triumph, blended
  With the winds, surround the world,
While we put their narrow beds in
  All who dared the right to prune;
With no scalp upon the red-skin,
  And serene and calm the moon.

THE BUFORD PIG.

I

COME listen, jolly suitors,
  A story I'll relate,
About a little Buford Pig
  And his untimely fate.
He'll never curl his tail again
  Across his bristly back,
Since overweight broke off the trade
  Between sweet Bill and Jack.

II

"*One twenty-five,*" his master said,
  Was *all* this pig should weigh;
The glutton filled his stomach full
  Of slop, and corn and hay,
Until, alas! when at the scales,
  This little pig alive
Brought down the beam quite easily
  At one and forty-five.

III

Indignant Bill refused to take
   This overgrown young pig;
One twenty-five the bargain was;
   'Tis *twenty* pounds too big.
The pig got mad and sued in court
   His wounded rights to claim;
He broke up Jack, he broke up Bill,
   And died a death of shame.

IV

His bristles made a dusting-brush,
   To clean Jack's pockets out;
His toe nails, sharpened to the quick,
   Tore William's bowels out;
And now his skin at Eckley's hangs,
   And it would make you laugh,
To see close by another skin,
   From Harvey's runty calf.

ALL ABOUT A PENNY.

I

Two neighbors had a lawsuit,
    And thus it came about:
Which note to place a credit on,
    That neither could find out.
Before a Justice both appeared,
    And had a trial fair;
The Justice found where it was due,
    And placed the credit there.

II

The man who gained the judgment
    With this was not content,
And said the Justice figured wrong,
    And lost to him a cent.
Straightway to court he did appeal,
    His missing cent to find,   ·
And found he had the costs to pay—
    That he had "gone it blind."

III

Take warning now; keep out of court,
  " Let well enough alone;"
Don't lose the substance out of spite,
  " To wrangle o'er a bone."
To save a cent and pay the costs
  Comes hardly with good grace;
"'Tis like the man who bit his nose
  From spite unto his face."

www.ingramcontent.com/pod-product-compliance
Lightning Source LLC
Chambersburg PA
CBHW021115020726
47500CB00003B/768